KATHY HENDERSON

The Storm

WALKER BOOKS
AND SUBSIDIARIES

LONDON • BOSTON • SYDNEY

Jim stood on the high grass bank
and stretched out his arms
like the sails of the windmill.

"All this is mine!"
he shouted at the wind.

Winter was nearly over.
The tide came in and the tide went out.

The beaches were empty and
flocks of geese gathered on the marshes.

Then
out of a great grey sky
the north wind
blew a gale.

All night long the wind raged.
It stirred up the sea, bent trees,
crashed tiles, smashed flowerpots,

rattled at the doors and windows
and tore through the dreams
of people sleeping.

The village sirens
wailed a flood warning.
Wake up!

Jim stumbled to the window
and looked out past the gate
and the road
and over the marsh
to the straight line
where the beach met the sky
just getting light.

What was that?
A splash of white.
Gone now.
No. It can't have been.
Yes! There's another
and another
bigger white wave
breaking over
the top of the beach
and pouring down
on to the land.

"Mum! Mum!
The sea! It's coming!"

Jim and his mother
ran in the dawn,
climbed the high grass bank
to try and see.
Up and up,
until the wind slapped their faces
and knocked them back.
One more step to
be able to look over...

But there was no over! The marsh had gone.
The windmill was surrounded and
in the distance where the beach had been

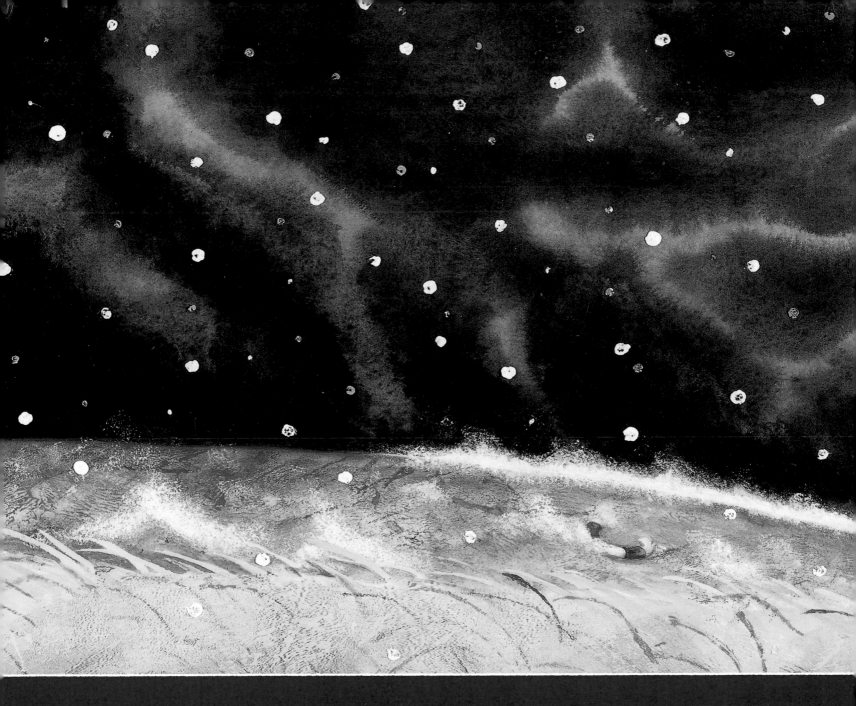

there was just a line of wild waves pounding.
"All this is mine!" roared the wind
and the sky hurled hail.

They ran for home,
stacked sandbags against the doors
and struggled up the hill
to Grandma's house.

"What shall we do
if the sea comes in?
Where shall we
go then?" asked Jim.

"Come in. Get warm.
You're safe up here.
The sea may rage
but the land is strong.
Come and we'll wait
for the tide to turn."

The wind rattled.
The radio chattered.
The clock in the hall ticked
as if nothing was the matter.

Ten past seven.
They sat and waited.
Half past seven was
crawling towards eight
when Jim called out,
"Oh look, Mum, look!
It's all right.
The water's going down!"

The storm had passed. Winter was nearly over.
Jim stood on the beach in the sun and
stretched out his arms
like the sails of
the windmill.

"All this is yours," he whispered to the wind and the sea lapped against the sand quiet as a lamb.